~> BOOK ELEVEN <~

ARACHNID
THE SPIDER KING

BY ADAM BLADE

ILLUSTRATED BY EZRA TUCKER

SCHOLASTIC INC.

New York Toronto London Auckland Sydney
Mexico City New Delhi Hong Kong Buenos Aires

With special thanks to Lucy Courtenay

For Sheila Noble

No part of this publication may be reproduced, stored in a retrieval system, or transmitted in any form or by any means, electronic, mechanical, photocopying, recording, or otherwise, without written permission of the publisher. For information regarding permission, write to Working Partners Ltd., Stanley House, St. Chad's Place, London WC1X 9HH, United Kingdom.

ISBN-13: 978-0-545-13265-7
ISBN-10: 0-545-13265-7

Beast Quest series created by Working Partners Ltd., London.
BEAST QUEST is a trademark of Working Partners Ltd.

Text © 2009 by Working Partners Ltd. All rights reserved.
Cover illustration © 2009 by David Wyatt

Published by Scholastic Inc., 557 Broadway, New York, NY 10012, by arrangement with Working Partners Ltd.

SCHOLASTIC, LITTLE APPLE, and associated logos are trademarks and/or registered trademarks of Scholastic Inc.

12 11 10 9 8 7   12 13 14/0

Designed by Tim Hall
Printed in the U.S.A.
First printing, May 2009

Did you think it was over?

Did you think I would accept defeat and disappear?

No! That can never be. I am Malvel, the Dark Wizard, who strikes fear into the hearts of the people of Avantia. I still have much more to show this wretched kingdom, and one boy in particular — Tom.

The young hero liberated the six Beasts of Avantia from my curse. But his fight is far from over. Let us see how he fares with a new Quest, one that will surely crush him and his companion, Elenna.

Avantia's Beasts had good hearts that I corrupted for my own wicked purpose. Now, thanks to Tom, they are free to protect the kingdom once more. But I have created new supreme Beasts whose hearts are evil and so cannot be set free. Each one guards a piece of the most precious relic of Avantia, a relic I have stolen: the suit of golden armor that gives magical strength to its rightful owner. I will stop at nothing to prevent Tom from collecting the complete suit and defeating me again. This time he will not win!

Malvel

T HE TWO WOMEN STOOD ON THE MOUNTAIN, gazing down into the cave. It gaped below them, dark and uninviting.

"Are you really going in, Etta?" said Dorina, the first woman.

Her friend nodded. "My father told me about this place," she said. "It's where you find the best crystals."

Dorina shivered. "I don't like it here," she said, glancing up at the dark forest above them.

"Don't worry," said Etta, tying a rope around her waist. "We are perfectly safe."

Dorina hugged herself. "My neighbor told me there were webs in her house this morning," she said. "Sticky ropes all over her bed. Don't pretend you aren't scared."

"If the spider is real, these crystals will protect us," said Etta firmly.

She lashed the other end of her rope to a nearby tree. Then she put a candle into a special holder and attached it to the leather cap she was wearing. With shaking hands, her friend lit the wick. Slowly, Etta lowered herself into the darkness.

"Be careful!" Dorina called after her.

The air inside the cave was musty and damp. Etta felt as if the mountain were pressing in on her, but she made herself go on. The candle in her cap flickered in the gloom. She could hear the nervous thump of her heart as she squeezed through the narrow channel of rock. The air grew colder as the cave opened up, and Etta gasped at the incredible sight before her.

The cave was like a cathedral. Huge stalactites hung from the roof, dripping icy water. Even larger stalagmites rose from the floor like church spires. Glistening blue crystals covered the walls.

"Dorina!" Etta called over her shoulder. "I've found them!"

Reaching for her pick, she began to chip at the crystals. A beautiful shard came away in her hand. Etta held it up to admire the way it sparkled in the candlelight.

Suddenly, the crystal's gleam seemed to cloud. Etta peered more closely at the shard and rubbed it on her sleeve. As she frowned in confusion, she felt something wet on her shoulder. She looked up.

A long string of saliva was dripping from a set of deadly fangs that loomed high above her.

Paralyzed with terror, Etta looked up into the six glittering eyes of an enormous black spider. His swaying shadow filled the cave.

The shard of crystal fell from Etta's hand. She opened her mouth to scream, but it was too late.

Thick ropes of silk fell on her like a net, pinning

her to the rock face. Struggling violently, Etta tried to free herself. It was no use. Faintly, she heard Dorina calling before the spider swiped at the rocks above and brought them tumbling down, blocking the cave's entrance.

Arachnid's hideous, hairy legs moved fast, spinning and whirling the silk around his victim. Then he scuttled back to the center of his mighty web.

Watching.

Waiting.

CHAPTER ONE

DESTINY!

Tom and Elenna watched Epos, the great flame bird of Avantia, soar into the glow of the setting sun.

"I can't believe we just rode on Epos," Elenna said, her eyes wide with excitement.

"Storm and Silver can't believe it, either." Tom grinned. "It's not every day that a stallion and a wolf ride a phoenix."

Storm shook his coal-black mane and nuzzled the silvery wolf at Elenna's side.

Tom removed his magical golden helmet and gazed at it with pride. He now had four pieces of Avantia's enchanted armor to help him in his quest to save his friend Aduro, King Hugo's wizard, who had been kidnapped by the evil wizard Malvel. The helmet granted Tom extra-keen sight, the chain mail gave him extra strength of heart in battle, the breastplate made him physically strong, and the leg armor allowed him to run fast over long distances. But there were still two pieces of armor to find, and they were protected by two more evil Beasts. Only when he and Elenna had defeated those Beasts could they vanquish Malvel and rescue Aduro.

Elenna handed him a flagon of water, and Tom drank deeply. The battle they had fought against Vipero the Snake Man in the desert was still on his mind. It had been the toughest test Tom had ever faced. But he had done it, with the help of his friends, and Tom had retrieved the golden leg armor. It was time for the next challenge.

"We have to go on," Tom said, returning the flagon to Elenna.

Storm whickered gently and pushed at Tom with his nose.

"No, Tom," said Elenna, her hand resting on Silver's back. "First we must rest."

"But Aduro needs our help more than ever!" Tom insisted. "We've got to find the next Beast!"

"You're tired," Elenna pointed out. "You need all your strength. You're no use to Aduro like this."

Tom knew his friend was right. Reluctantly, he set up camp while Elenna built a fire.

Almost as soon as the sun had vanished over the horizon, a chill creeped into the air. Tom and Elenna ate bread and cheese and drank water from a nearby stream. Storm cropped the grass, and Silver padded silently into the darkness, bringing back two rabbits.

"We'll leave first thing in the morning," said Tom, studying his enchanted map in the firelight. "The map is showing a road that will take us toward the mountains, where the next piece of armor is waiting for us."

"Perfect." Elenna yawned, settling down. "Try to sleep now."

Tom gazed at the four pieces of golden armor, glowing in the light of the campfire next to the sword and shield given to him by Aduro. Shuddering, Tom remembered the vision Malvel had shown them of the good wizard.

Aduro, his friend and protector, had been bound to a chair that dangled dangerously above a pit of gurgling, spluttering tar. Malvel had told Tom that every time he lost heart, the good wizard would be lowered closer to the boiling tar.

He swallowed. He couldn't let his friend down. But doubts still swarmed through his mind. Malvel had told them that the next Beast was a monstrous spider. It sounded terrifying.

How could he and Elenna fight a creature like that?

Tom tossed and turned on the hard ground, exhausted but unable to sleep. Then he sensed Storm above him. The stallion snorted, gently blowing Tom's hair away from his face. Feeling comforted, Tom closed his eyes and felt his heart lighten. He had succeeded in so many Quests already. He could surely complete another one.

Tom slept deeply. When he awoke the next morning, the sun was peeping over the horizon. He drew on his new leg armor, feeling an instant pulse of energy.

"You take Storm," he suggested to Elenna as they packed up their belongings after breakfast. "My leg armor makes me feel as if I could run forever."

"Sounds like a good idea to me," Elenna laughed.

She climbed onto Storm's back and settled into the saddle. Then she clicked her tongue and kicked her heels. The stallion whinnied and broke into a gallop.

Wearing the leg armor, Tom found that he could easily keep up. His legs felt like giant springs. He sprinted beside Elenna and Storm, whooping with pleasure as the wind buffeted his face. Silver raced beside him, leaping and barking with delight.

"Look, Tom!" said Elenna. "An orchard!"

Gnarled apple trees groaning with fruit stood at the side of the road, near a lively stream. Tom sprang for the nearest tree, landing easily on a branch near the bottom. He reached for the apples and dropped them down to Elenna, before hopping back to the ground. The apples were crisp and cool, and juice ran down Tom's and Elenna's chins as they bit into them. Storm hungrily tore apples from the branches, while Silver bounded between the trees and rolled in the long grass.

"I never knew an apple could taste so delicious," Tom said, grinning.

Elenna laughed. "Nor did Storm!" she said. "I think he's eaten about twenty."

Tom felt a surge of gratitude for his three friends. They had come so far together already. With Elenna, Storm, and Silver by his side, Tom felt he could fight twenty Beasts.

As he rested against the tree, Tom suddenly saw, out of the corner of his eye, the initial *T* carved into the ancient bark. He traced the letter with his fingers, his heart thumping. Could it mean Taladon? He felt a mixture of sadness and excitement, as he always did when he thought of the father he had never met.

"Look, Elenna," he said. "*T* for Taladon! Perhaps

he passed this way. Perhaps . . ." His voice trailed into nothing.

"You'll see him one day," said Elenna, guessing instantly what was on Tom's mind.

Tom smiled at his friend. He hoped with all his heart that she was right.

He pulled his enchanted map and then his magical compass from Storm's saddlebag and studied them carefully. He had been given the compass by his uncle, who had told him that the compass once belonged to Tom's father. The needle showed him when to step forward to meet his destiny, and when to flee impossible danger. Tom held the compass tightly, then placed it on the map, which once again came to life. Mountains rose up in miniature, rivers gleamed, and tiny trees swayed in the wind. A glowing red line appeared, showing Tom the way to a town that nestled at the edge of the mountains. Right next to the town, near a rocky outcrop, a pair of minuscule golden gauntlets glittered. The next piece of armor! Tom swiveled the compass until the needle pointed toward the town.

Destiny, it read.

Tom rolled up the map and gathered his courage.

"It's time to fight a giant spider!" he said.

→ CHAPTER TWO ←

A PARTY

TIRED AND HUNGRY AFTER A LONG JOURNEY, Tom, Elenna, Storm, and Silver came at last to the town. It was surrounded by gray, forbidding walls, the same color as the mountains that stood behind it.

To Tom and Elenna's surprise, throngs of people were moving through the main gates.

"I wonder what's happening here today?" Tom said, looking around.

"Market day, perhaps," Elenna said.

The smell of freshly baked bread wafted toward them. Tom's stomach rumbled. They hadn't had a good meal for several days, and the thought of food and a soft bed was very appealing.

They followed the crowds and entered the town. Colored streamers hung merrily from the windows of houses. Flags lined the streets, rippling in the cool mountain breeze. Market traders were selling toys and trinkets, and jugglers performed on street corners. Everywhere Tom and Elenna looked, there was music and laughter. People pushed and jostled, calling out to one another in cheerful voices. The street soon opened into a brightly decorated town square. Wooden tables and benches lined the marketplace, and the smell of hot stew filled the air.

"Come, friends!" laughed a trader, offering Tom and Elenna shiny candied apples. "Two pennies each. Long live the King!"

"Of course!" said Elenna. "It's the King's birthday. Everyone in Avantia will be celebrating."

Tom quickly found a tethering post for Storm.

"Hungry, are you?" He laughed at Silver, who had pounced on a chicken drumstick that had been thrown to the ground. "I know how you feel!"

"Join us, travelers!" called out a jolly-faced man at a nearby table. "There's plenty for all who call themselves friends of King Hugo!"

Tom and Elenna settled down on a bench and helped themselves to stew and bread. Silver sat at Elenna's feet, patiently gnawing his chicken bone.

The Quest was still on Tom's mind, but he ate hungrily, watching and listening to the people around him. Although the merriment that filled the town was infectious, he noticed several uneasy faces and wondered if the townspeople were aware that an evil Beast lived so close to them.

"Do you think they know about the spider?" he asked Elenna, leaning close.

She shook her head. "Why should they? To most people in Avantia, the Beasts are just myths."

After the meal, the tables were cleared away and games began. An archery target was set up on one side of the square, and a children's coconut shy on the other. The street entertainers were now in the middle of the marketplace, and the townspeople danced while red-faced town musicians played their instruments.

"Come and try the coconut shy," Elenna said, dragging Tom from his seat. "Look at the prizes!"

Lined up on the wooden table beside the coconut shy were a number of small creatures made of clay.

"It's Tartok!" Tom gasped, recognizing the famous Beast. The last time he had seen the snow monster had been on the icy plains in the North, where he had freed her from Malvel's evil curse.

"See what I mean," said Elenna. "These people think the Beasts of Avantia are just fairy tales, fit for children's toys."

She seized three balls. Winking at Tom, she

let them fly toward the coconuts, one after the other.

Thump, thump, thump. Three coconuts fell to the ground.

The crowd cheered.

"That was brilliant, miss," said a small boy, watching as Elenna collected three little Tartoks from the stallholder.

"Thanks," said Elenna. "Here!" She tossed the boy one of the toys.

"Thanks!" the boy shouted happily.

Tom watched as he scampered off, clutching his prize. It had been such a long time since he had been able to play with toys or have fun at a street festival. The Quest had taken over his life.

"You get an extra prize for knocking off three coconuts, miss," the stallholder said to Elenna.

"Do I?" Elenna said, laughing, as she gave away her last two Tartoks to an excited little girl and her brother. "What is it?"

"A wish," said the stallholder with a smile. "Anything you fancy. Within reason, of course."

"Well, that's easy," said Elenna, patting Silver as he frolicked around her feet. "What I wish for is a long sleep on a comfortable mattress."

"We've been traveling for a long time," Tom explained. He wondered what he would say if the stallholder asked them where they were going. Their Quest was a secret, after all.

But the man simply nodded. Then a voice came from behind them.

"I have a spare room in my house."

Tom turned to see a tall, thin woman with dark hair. She didn't return his smile.

"That would be wonderful," said Elenna. "Thank you."

"I am Dorina," the woman said. "Please come with me."

She turned and walked away, her head down. She didn't look at the entertainers or musicians as they passed. Tom and Elenna glanced at each other. It was clear that Dorina was in no mood for celebrations. Tom felt a lurch in his stomach. Perhaps this was what he had been looking for — someone who knew that danger lurked.

"Your town is very welcoming," Tom said, hurrying to catch up with her. "Have you enjoyed the festivities?"

Dorina stopped. "I have lost my friend," she said. "There is nothing for me to celebrate." Tears filled her eyes. "Etta went into the mountain caves," she said. "I was there. I watched as she . . ." Her voice choked.

"What happened?" Elenna said.

"She didn't come back," Dorina whispered, wiping the tears from her eyes. "She went in search of the crystals that protect us. But there was some kind of earthquake. Rocks fell and blocked the entrance to the caves."

Tom's skin tingled. Was this the Beast's work?

"Why do you need protection?" he asked.

"There is a giant spider living in the high forests," Dorina sniffed. "I've heard he is called Arachnid." Tom and Elenna shivered. "The blue crystals in the caves are said to protect us. But strange things are happening in our town. Huge webs are spun around the walls in the night, and food is disappearing. Don't let these festivities fool you. We are all scared. We know that when the food is gone, the spider will come for *us* — and there is nothing we can do!"

Daylight was fading. A pale moon peeped out from behind the clouds, then vanished again. The mountains above the town looked vast and dark. Tom stared up at them. He could see the fringes of a great forest on the upper slopes, black and forbidding in the dusk. Somewhere among those distant trees, the Beast was waiting for Tom, guarding the fifth piece of precious golden armor. Tom knew that to protect its prize, Malvel's evil Beast would give its life.

Would Tom have to risk his own life to retrieve the golden gauntlets?

CHAPTER THREE

SPIDER IN THE NIGHT

COME ON," ELENNA SAID, GENTLY PLACING A hand on Tom's shoulder. "We need a good night's sleep if we're going to face Arachnid."

Tom fetched Storm from his tethering post. They followed Dorina to her house, in a side street near the marketplace. Tom settled Storm in Dorina's stable, then followed Elenna and Silver into the house.

The air inside smelled of beeswax and lavender. The furniture looked well polished and the windows gleamed.

"I hope you will be comfortable," said Dorina,

showing them into her spare room at the back of the house.

Two fat, hay-filled mattresses lay on wooden beds, scenting the room with a clean, grassy smell. The view from the window looked onto the small yard and stables beyond. Everything was shrouded in darkness.

"I could sleep for a week," Elenna groaned, flopping onto one of the mattresses. Silver curled up underneath the bed and settled his silvery head on his paws.

"There will be supper on the table later," said Dorina. "If you wish it." She bowed her head and left the room, softly shutting the door behind her.

Something about Dorina's story worried Tom. After fighting ten Beasts, his instincts were starting to tell him when things weren't right.

"Do you think Arachnid has got Dorina's

friend?" he asked, kicking off his boots and sitting on his own mattress.

Elenna looked surprised. "The spider is supposed to live in the forest high up on the mountainside," she said. "Not in the caves near the town."

"I have a feeling that Arachnid is closer than everyone thinks," said Tom grimly. "Remember what Dorina said about the webs in the town? And the way the food disappears every night? And yet no one ever sees this spider. It's a long way down to the town from the mountaintops. Isn't it more likely that the spider has moved closer to his source of food, and set up home in the nearby caves?"

Elenna looked uneasy. "You may be right," she said.

Tom thumped his hand on the mattress. "We have to find Arachnid," he said. "We have to defeat him and rescue Dorina's friend. Before it's too late!"

"Hmm," mumbled Elenna sleepily. Her eyes were fluttering and closing.

Tom wanted to go straight to the caves. But watching Elenna, he remembered how little they had slept in the past few days. She was already breathing peacefully, curled up on her soft hay mattress. It wasn't fair to drag her out into the night — not now.

Tom felt too tense to sleep. Instead, he settled down beside the window. He would keep watch. If the spider came in the night, Tom would be the first to know.

Tom woke suddenly. His neck was stiff, his arms wrapped around his knees. With dismay, he realized that he had fallen asleep on the floor by the window.

The weak moon shone into the room, filling it with a soft, misty glow. Everything was still and silent. But Silver was growling softly, his eyes bright in the moonlight. Tom glanced at Elenna, still fast asleep. Then he saw a pulsing light coming from the saddlebag on the floor.

Tom stood up stiffly and reached for his bag. He pulled out the magical map. The red path showing them the way to the mountains seemed to be glowing with extra urgency. They were running out of time.

Silver was still growling. His body was tense, ready to spring.

"Shush, boy," Tom whispered. Then he noticed something strange about the moonlight. It was as if the moon were shining through a veil of some kind. With a shiver of disgust, he saw a thick spiderweb had been woven across the window.

With a mounting sense of horror, Tom gazed around the room, swiveling slowly to take it all in. Every surface was covered with gauzy webs. He backed away from the window — and found

himself entangled in a prison of clammy, silken threads.

"Arghh!" Tom yelled in shock, lashing out.

Elenna sat up in bed, startled by Tom's yell. "Yuck!" she exclaimed, tearing at the thick, sticky ropes that twisted over her sheets and blankets.

"Arachnid has been here," Tom said urgently, pulling on the four pieces of golden armor. "In this room with us, Elenna! There's no time to waste. We have to leave for the mountains at once!"

He showed Elenna the map. Wide awake now, Elenna pushed her way through the webs surrounding her bed.

"This is awful," she whispered, her face pale. "We have to do something."

The floor was tacky underfoot. Tom grimaced in disgust as he reached for the lamp beside his bed and lit the wick. Quietly, they tiptoed out of the bedroom, with Silver padding silently beside Elenna.

There was no sign of a light beneath Dorina's door as they creeped past. Webs hung from the polished banisters and formed thick curtains over the walls. There was something beautiful about the way they twisted and spiraled, glistening softly in the lamplight — and yet something deadly, too. They brushed at Tom's cheeks as he and Elenna hurried down the stairs.

"I'll leave some money in thanks," said Elenna in a low voice. "I don't want Dorina to think that we left in the night like thieves."

She took two candles from the pantry, and left a small pile of coins.

"At least the townspeople are still asleep," Tom whispered to Elenna as they led Storm out of his stable. "No one needs to know about our Quest. We can leave the town and climb the mountains by daybreak."

Just then a hand grasped his shoulder. Tom cried out.

"What are you doing?" Dorina asked, her eyes wild and frightened as she pulled a thick woolen blanket around her shoulders to ward off the night chill. "Where are you going?"

"We have urgent business," Elenna said.

"The spider came in the night," Dorina whispered. "You saw its webs. We are all lost unless you find it and kill it."

Tom gasped. How did she know about their Quest?

"You are going to find it, aren't you?" Dorina said to Tom. Her eyes were huge in the moonlight. "I watched you in the town square today. You were looking for something. You are not ordinary travelers. I can see that by your armor. Please — tell me. I must know!"

Tom had to tell her the truth. "We are," he said.

"We think it's in the caves. But swear that you will tell no one!"

"I swear," Dorina said fiercely. "The tunnel Etta used is blocked now, but there is another entrance to the caves farther up the mountain. The path is dangerous, but keep your back to the mountainside and you will make it. And take this; it will help you."

She pushed something cold and hard into Tom's hand. It was a shard of glittering blue crystal.

"Go," she said, backing away. "And may the Beasts of Avantia be with you!"

→ CHAPTER FOUR ←

A LONG WAY DOWN

TOM EXAMINED THE CRYSTAL AS STORM BLEW softly over his shoulder. It was certainly pretty, reminding him of a sapphire.

"That's not protection," Elenna snorted, slinging the saddlebags over Storm's back. "That's jewelry."

As he put the crystal in his pocket and gave Elenna a leg up onto Storm, Tom had to agree with her. He had more faith in his shield and armor than in a shiny piece of blue glass.

The candles and the red glow from the map lit their way out of the town. Thick silver webs were draped everywhere. Several unwary rats and mice struggled, caught in the silken tangles. Tom tried not to think about the size of the spider that had spun them.

The road out of town was straight and well surfaced. But as they approached the bottom of the mountain, it began to change. Soon, even Tom was struggling in his magical leg armor, and Storm lost his footing several times on loose shingle. Tom shifted his shield onto his back and used his hands to steady himself, skirting puddles that gleamed in the moonlight. The sky was getting lighter. Sunrise wasn't far away.

The road dwindled to a track, growing steeper with every passing minute. Tom was glad of his golden helmet. He could see the dangers underfoot, as well as the mountain track that twisted ahead of them.

They reached the rocky outcrop marked on the map just as the sun broke over the horizon.

"This must be where Etta entered the caves,"

said Elenna, stooping down and peering into the dark hole in the mountainside. "I can see the rocks blocking the way." She shuddered. "How terrible to be trapped down there."

"The map is showing us the other entrance," said Tom, showing Elenna the glowing red line. They looked up the mountainside to where the path snaked out of sight.

"Is that the only way?" Elenna said in dismay.

Dorina had warned them the path was dangerous. But it looked impossibly narrow, and to the right was a sheer drop.

"We'll be fine," Tom said.

Storm tossed his head nervously. Undeterred, Tom took the stallion's reins and led him forward.

Elenna hung back. "Tom," she said in a choked voice. "I can't do this."

Silver nuzzled Elenna's hand comfortingly.

"You and I have fought ten Beasts," said Tom. "You can walk this path, Elenna. Trust me."

Hesitantly, Elenna began to follow him.

They reached the point where the path wrapped itself around the edge of the mountain. There was no turning back now.

"It's a long way down," Elenna said, looking over the edge.

There was barely room for one person to pass, and in places, the path had crumbled away.

"You go first. Keep your back to the mountain," Tom instructed. "You can lean into it and use it as a support."

They took turns to move down the path. Elenna slid along with her back to the mountain and her eyes straight ahead. Silver picked his way behind her, as sure-footed as ever. Seizing Storm's reins, Tom clicked his tongue. "Come on, boy," he said. "We can do this!"

Tom inched along the path, leading Storm and trying not to look down. But he felt the path disintegrating. Stones bounced away and disappeared over the edge of the mountain. He moved a little faster. More stones fell.

"The path is collapsing! Run, Tom!" Elenna shouted in front of him.

Tom ran. Storm whinnied in terror, racing close behind him. Stumbling and slipping, Tom could feel the path crumbling behind them. Could they make it before the path fell away completely?

Tom's feet suddenly met air. His heart crashed in his chest as he grabbed at the mountainside. But the stones came away in his fist. There was nothing he could do. He was going to fall!

Instinctively, he let go of Storm's reins. He could hear Elenna scream as he plunged over the edge. Then her voice was snatched away in the wind. The mountainside was racing past in a blur. Tom wrestled with the shield strapped to his back and

pulled it over his head. The gift from Cypher — a single tear from the giant's eye — that was set into his shield protected him from falling. At once, he felt himself slowing. He angled the shield so that he could float close enough to the mountainside to find something to hold on to and stop his fall.

At last his hand closed around a spur of rock. Tom closed his eyes. *Thank goodness!* he thought. Opening his eyes again, he looked up at the path overhead. It was a stiff climb back to the others. Steadying himself with his feet, he slung his shield back over his shoulder and began to make his way up. The golden breastplate pulsed strength into his chest and his legs, helping him.

Elenna was waiting for him, tense and white-faced. She helped Tom to pull himself over the edge and back onto solid ground, where he collapsed in a patch of scrubby grass.

"I thought you'd gone forever!" Elenna burst out when Tom had got his breath back.

"You can't lose me that easily," Tom said.

Elenna laughed in relief. Then she looked more serious. "There's no way back," she said. "I pulled Storm across just in time. The path has completely disappeared."

It was true. Where the path had been was now a yawning chasm.

"We'll worry about that after we've defeated Arachnid," Tom said.

He thought about the golden gauntlets. Would the spider be guarding them in his web? Tom shivered, but he knew that he couldn't lose heart. Only by winning all six pieces of the armor could he save Aduro from Malvel's evil clutches.

It was now or never.

The Beast was waiting.

CHAPTER FIVE

ARACHNID'S LAIR

TOM STOOD AT THE MOUTH OF THE CAVE. THEY hadn't had to walk much farther to find it. It looked narrow and gloomy. Storm shifted restlessly, sniffing the stale air within.

"Are you ready?" Tom asked Elenna over his shoulder.

"Ready as I'll ever be," said Elenna, stroking the top of Silver's head. She took the candles from her pack and a flint from her pocket. With a steady hand, she struck the flint and lit the wicks. Then she passed a candle to Tom.

Tom held it above his head and led the way. Storm and Silver followed, with Elenna bringing up the rear, holding the second candle. It wasn't long before they'd left the daylight behind.

The cave floor sloped sharply. Skidding on the loose stones, Tom put his hand out. The walls were slippery and sparkled dimly under his fingers. Tom realized that they were studded with blue crystals.

He could hear Storm snorting nervously and Silver whining as they descended.

A cold gust of wind suddenly blew out the candles. Even though he was wearing his magical helmet, Tom could see nothing. Would they have to continue their journey in darkness?

As Tom's eyes grew used to the gloom, he stared at the walls of the tunnel in surprise. They were glowing!

"The crystals, Tom!" Elenna whispered, reaching up to touch the blue gems. "They've taken the light from our candles and are reflecting it back at us!"

They are protecting us after all, Tom thought.

The path took them around a narrow corner and into a vast, echoing cave. Tom stared in amazement at the space around them. Vast stalactites hung from the roof, and stalagmites grew up from the floor. The air was damp and cool, and filled with the sound of dripping water.

Tom felt a chill in his bones. He was sure the Beast was close.

He stepped farther into the cave. There was a rasping hiss from somewhere in the gloom. Then something whisked through the air toward him and grasped his waist. Looking down, Tom saw a thick rope of spider silk had wrapped around him. He tried to pull against it, but the thread grew tighter, constricting his breathing.

He was right. Arachnid was in the cave!

There was another hiss. A second jet of silk landed on Elenna with deadly accuracy.

"Help!" Elenna screamed, struggling to free herself.

Silver growled and seized the web with his teeth, but it only made things worse.

"Struggling will make it tighter," said Tom, trying to remain calm. "Stay still."

Elenna stopped struggling and steadied her breathing. She tried instead to soothe her frightened wolf. Silver growled softly.

Storm tried to back out of the cave.

"It's all right, boy," said Tom, holding the reins tightly.

The stallion calmed a little, but pawed the ground with his hooves.

Elenna carefully freed herself from the sticky web. It was difficult to untangle and clung to her hair and clothes.

There was another hiss, dark and deadly-sounding. Tom was ready this time, leaping out of the way as another jet hurtled toward him. He looked around. Where was Arachnid?

In the darkest part of the cave, a ghastly sight

met his eyes. Sitting in the middle of an enormous web that stretched right across a cavern was a gigantic spider.

Arachnid was the size of a barn. Eight hairy legs protruded from his body, waving lazily in the air. Thick saliva dripped from his long, sharp fangs, and he watched Tom carefully with six evil eyes. The Beast opened his jaw and moaned. The putrid smell of death filled the air.

Silver barked ferociously as Tom tried to see what lay beneath Arachnid's web. The cavern looked dark and bottomless.

"Look beside the spider," said Elenna in a low voice.

The golden gauntlets were sitting in the heart of the web. They were the same burnished gold as the rest of Tom's enchanted armor, and were molded in the shape of two paws with long talons arching over each finger.

Without meaning to, Tom took a step forward. His feet crunched on something and he looked down. Scattered on the floor were piles of leathery old spider skins that Arachnid had shed. Then he realized in horror that the giant spider was drawing him in, tugging with deadly purpose on the sticky silk around his waist.

Arachnid reared back furiously. For the first time, Tom saw the spider's most deadly weapons. On the spider's underbelly were rows and rows of sharp teeth. The spider's monstrous legs were whirling, gathering in his web — and his victims.

They were going to be eaten alive!

CHAPTER SIX

THE GOLDEN GAUNTLETS

THE GIANT SPIDER LET OUT ANOTHER HIGH-pitched moan that echoed off the walls of the cave. The sound chilled Tom to the bone. Then the Beast brought his long legs back down to his web. Tom felt behind for his shield and pulled it across his body to protect himself from further jets. Then he drew his sword and slashed through the web around his waist.

Thanks to his magical helmet, Tom could see every hair on Arachnid's ugly body. He also could see himself reflected in the spider's six eyes. The Beast was watching Tom's every move.

Tom readied himself for the spider's attack. But Arachnid didn't shift. He was guarding the treasure that lay in the heart of his web.

Another spurt of silk whistled toward Tom. Just in time, Tom lifted his shield.

Still crouched beside the gauntlets, the spider lunged at Tom with one long black leg. Tom thrust hard with his sword. The blade bounced off the spider's skin. Elenna loosed an arrow, but it clattered against Arachnid and fell uselessly into the web.

"His hide is too tough," Tom panted.

How were they going to defeat this evil Beast?

"Look up, Tom!" Elenna called. "The stalactites!"

The rows of jagged stalactites clung to the cave roof, their sharp points deadly and still dripping with the water that had formed them over millions of years. If a stalactite fell, Tom knew that any of them could be killed instantly.

"That's it!" Tom gasped. "If I can break a stalactite from the roof, I can use it as a spear!"

He sheathed his sword and reached for a handhold on the smooth wall. Arachnid hissed with rage as Tom began to pull himself up toward the nearest stalactite, his feet scrabbling for a foothold. It was impossible. The walls were too slippery. He fell back to the floor.

The giant spider began to move reluctantly away from the center of his web. The gauntlets gleamed in the dim light. Tom thought of Aduro being lowered toward Malvel's deadly pit of tar. He had to get the gauntlets or die in the attempt!

Tom felt Storm push him gently with his nose. It gave him an idea. Could he use the stallion to reach a stalactite?

"Here, boy," said Tom, coaxing Storm closer to the cave wall.

Seeing what Tom was trying to do, Elenna ran to help, with Silver by her side. Tom put his foot in Storm's stirrup, and Elenna gave him a leg up onto the stallion's back. Then Tom stood on the well-worn leather saddle and reached up. His fingers brushed the rough, pointed tip of a stalactite. If he could just grasp it —

Arachnid hissed and reared again.

Storm whinnied in terror and jumped forward, despite Elenna's best efforts to hold him still.

Tom grasped desperately at the stalactite, thrown off balance by Storm's sudden movement. It was too late! The rock slipped from his fingers, and Tom began to fall.

There wasn't time to lift his shield above his head to protect himself from the fall. Whistling through the cold air, Tom landed on something soft. He looked beneath him, and his heart thudded in his chest.

He had landed in Arachnid's web.

Tom could feel the deadly strength of the sticky fibers. He needed all the strength of his magical breastplate to pull himself loose. Arachnid began to move in Tom's direction, his six eyes narrowing in the pleasure of the hunt. Tom struggled desperately to stay upright as the web rocked beneath him. He stretched out his hand to keep his balance, then pulled it back as the gluey ropes sucked at his fingers.

Another jet of silken thread hurtled toward Tom just as he ripped himself free from the web and threw himself past the spider at the golden gauntlets.

Arachnid shrieked with rage. Tom had only seconds before the spider would attack again. He grabbed the gauntlets and thrust his hands inside them. At once, his fingers tingled with new strength and twitched toward his scabbard. Tom instantly realized that the gauntlets would give him special skills with his sword!

He pulled the sword from its sheath. It felt like a living thing in his hands, ready to do his every

bidding. The chain mail tingled around his chest, filling him with courage. With five pieces of armor and the five magical gifts they bestowed upon him, Tom knew he could defeat the spider. He whirled the sword above his head and brought it down on the silken ropes that clung to his feet.

At once, a gap opened between Tom and the spider. But without the web, there was nothing to stop Tom from falling into the bottomless cavern beneath!

The giant spider scuttled to safety at the edge of the web as Tom fell through the hole. For the second time that day, he pulled his shield over his head. Immediately, he felt his fall slowing, and he thanked Cypher the Mountain Giant for the token that gave the shield that particular power. It gave him just enough time to reach out and grab hold of the cavern wall.

Quickly, he began to climb back up to Elenna,

Storm, and Silver. He had to protect them! Arachnid could attack at any moment.

His heart was thundering in his ears as he hauled himself up. His legs were growing weak from the climb, and he knew that his armor was helping him to make the ascent this time. His breastplate gave him the strength he needed to pull himself upward. His legs, encased in their special leg armor, pushed him steadily on. He could feel his strength and purpose returning as the magic of Avantia wrapped its protection around him. His friends were waiting for him. He wouldn't let them down!

Elenna looked over the edge of the cavern as Tom pulled himself to the top.

Behind Elenna, Tom saw Silver. And behind Silver, the shadow of the spider was looming, his fangs dripping.

CHAPTER SEVEN

THE BATTLE BEGINS

SILVER!" TOM CRIED.

Elenna whirled around. But it was too late. Arachnid had pulled the wolf into his web. Silver struggled, but he was trapped.

"No!" Elenna shouted.

Arachnid's legs reached for the wolf. Silver snarled up at the giant spider. He bared his sharp teeth and swiped at the Beast with his claws. But Arachnid ignored him. He began to spin ropes of silvery thread, wrapping the wolf up like a parcel. Growling and snapping, Silver fought back. But his struggles made things worse as the web wound more tightly around him. It was no use. He couldn't free himself.

Tom felt a surge of anger. He couldn't let Silver lose his life! Then he remembered the stalactites. He ran to the edge of the cave, his leg armor throbbing with magical energy. He leaped up and onto the wall. This time the gauntlets gave him extra grip as he hauled himself up toward the stalactites. He moved across the cave wall, foothold by foothold. Then he stretched himself as far as he could. A deadly-looking stalactite was almost within reach!

By now, Arachnid had almost finished his vile work. Thick threads were wound around Silver's whole body. The wolf's growls and snarls were growing fainter.

"Quickly, Tom!" Elenna cried, her voice cracking. She was kneeling at the edge of the web, reaching helplessly toward her wolf. "I don't think

Silver can last much longer!" In despair, she pulled an arrow from her quiver and loosed it at the spider. It clattered uselessly away.

Tom moved farther up the wall until his head touched the cave roof. He was holding on by his fingertips. How could he go on? The armor was giving him magical skills, but it was also heavy, dragging his body down.

Then Tom felt the breastplate fill him with fresh energy and the chain mail give him strength of heart. He could not fail! Grunting with the effort, he gripped the wall with one hand and reached for his sword. It slid swiftly from its scabbard. He swiped fiercely at the root of the stalactite. The jagged rock shuddered, but didn't come away.

Even with the magical skills of the gauntlets, Tom found it difficult to aim his sword at the right angle from his position near the roof. He twisted his body, reaching his arm as far as he could. Again

and again, he hacked at the stalactite, his muscles screaming in agony. Sweat ran into his eyes, making it difficult to see.

Down below, he could see Arachnid toying with Silver, batting him back and forth across the web. It wouldn't be long before the Beast grew tired of his game. . . .

Then Elenna screamed.

"Look, Tom!" she said, pointing.

Tom peered into the far corner of the cave. Something else was trussed up in the web. Something that was moaning and wriggling.

It came to Tom in a flash. Etta, Dorina's friend!

"We're coming, Etta!" Tom shouted. He hacked again at the stalactite. "Don't give up hope!"

The wolf had stopped fighting now. He lay still at Arachnid's feet.

"Silver!" Elenna called, as Storm snorted and tossed his long black mane. "Oh, Silver, hold on!"

Arachnid moaned. The venom on his fangs gleamed. Tom hesitated. Both Silver and Etta needed his help! But there was so little time.

Even with his five pieces of magical armor, Tom knew that he couldn't do this on his own. It was time to call upon one of the good Beasts of Avantia. Who might be able to help him?

Then, thinking back to the toys at the fair, the answer came to him: Tartok.

The last time Tom had seen the great Ice Beast had been on the edge of the northern icy plains. He could only hope that the Beast would come to his aid now.

Sheathing his sword, Tom continued to grip on to the cave wall and reached around his back to touch Tartok's claw, which was set deep into his shield.

Almost instantly, he heard a mighty roar.

The Beast had come!

CHAPTER EIGHT

TARTOK TO THE RESCUE

PART OF THE CAVE WALL CAME CRASHING down, revealing dazzling daylight as the snow monster thundered inside. The ground trembled.

"Tartok!" Tom cried in relief.

Seizing Storm's reins, Elenna ran beneath a rocky overhang as rocks bounced around the cave floor. Tom clung to his position near the roof as Tartok leaped across the web toward the great spider.

Arachnid screamed and reared. The razor-sharp teeth on his belly glinted in the bright sunshine. He shot ropes of silk straight at the Beast, who shook them off as if they were flies. There was a flash of Tartok's claws, and an unearthly screech from the spider. Tom gasped. Tartok had slashed into Arachnid's six eyes, blinding the spider!

"Now, Elenna!" Tom roared. "Save Silver! I'll cut Etta free!"

The giant spider shrieked and thumped at the cave walls with his legs. Tartok growled and beat her chest. In the chaos, Elenna dashed from her rocky hiding place and leaped across the web, bouncing and staggering on its sticky threads. With her knife, she slashed at the silk that bound the wolf, then dragged Silver away from the web's deadly embrace to the safety of the cave floor.

"Silver," Elenna sobbed, throwing her arms around the wolf's shaggy neck as he gently licked her arm. "I'm so glad you're safe."

Tom whistled for Storm, who cantered from beneath the overhang. Then Tom dropped onto the stallion's back. Storm whinnied in triumph.

Whirling his sword, Tom turned Storm toward Etta and dug his heels into the stallion's sides.

Storm cantered across the uneven rocks, bounding over the cracks and crevasses. The cave was shaking as the two great Beasts fought. Arachnid was lunging and snapping, fighting with all eight legs, as Tartok swiped the air with her fearsome claws.

Tom threw himself from the saddle and scrambled across to Etta. The cave walls groaned. Cracks appeared, snaking from the floor to the roof as pebbles rained down from the ceiling. They didn't have much time. The woman was bound so tightly that all Tom could see was a pair of terrified eyes staring out at him. How would he free her without cutting her with his sword?

Trusting to the skill of his gauntlets to help him, Tom let his sword fly. His aim felt truer than it had ever been. *Slash! Slash!*

"Thank you, oh thank you," Etta sobbed as the web fell away from her. "How can I repay you? How —"

"Tom!" Elenna screamed. "The roof is falling in!"

"Take the animals to safety, Elenna!" he shouted. "Go with my friend," he said to Etta. "She will keep you safe."

"But wh-wh-what are you going to do?" stammered Etta.

"Fight the Beast," Tom said grimly.

Elenna grabbed Etta by the hand and ran for the fresh hole in the cave wall created by Tartok's entrance. Silver raced at her side. The ground shuddered as the Beasts swayed and struck at one another. Even without sight, Arachnid was matching Tartok blow for blow. The spider's razor-like teeth tore into Tartok's flesh, scattering red blood on the rocks. *What if Tartok was unable to defeat this monster?* Tom wondered. If it was too much for a great Beast of Avantia, then what chance did he have?

But Tom knew that every time he faltered, Aduro would be lowered even closer to Malvel's pit of tar. He had to stay strong, for Aduro's sake! If he could just return to that stalactite and tear it free . . .

Tom leaped back onto Storm. Bending low over the stallion's neck, he galloped back to the stalactite he had tried to break away from the cave roof. Storm skidded to a halt as Tom scrambled to his feet on the stallion's broad back. He tensed his muscles and once more felt the golden leg armor fill his legs with strength. Then he jumped.

Soaring over the heads of the fighting Beasts, Tom landed hard on the stalactite, the golden gauntlets helping him to grip. The stalactite shuddered, jarred by the impact. Tom could see a crack forming where the calcite spear joined the roof. He drew his sword and hacked at the crack.

"One more blow," Tom panted, striking madly again and again. "Just one more . . ."

There was a groan as the stalactite tore away from the roof and fell — with Tom still clinging to it.

With a resounding crunch, the stalactite plunged into Arachnid's back. The Beast let out a roar of pain. Tom threw himself free as the spider arched his vile black body in agony, hurling himself around the cave, trying to get the stalactite out. But every time the Beast struck a wall, the impact drove the stalactite deeper into his flesh.

At last, the huge spider gave one final roar and disappeared.

In his place, thousands of tiny spiders skittered madly across the rocks. Arachnid had been defeated!

But Tom had no time to celebrate. A huge *boom* sounded above him, and great chunks of rock began to fall from the walls. Chasms opened at Tom's feet. Everything was collapsing.

"Tartok!" Tom yelled, pulling himself to his feet. "We must get out of here before it's too late!"

The great Ice Beast roared.

Tom ran for daylight as the mountain caved in.

CHAPTER NINE

STAY STRONG!

TOM HURLED HIMSELF OUTSIDE, ROCKS cascading around him. The whole mountainside seemed to be falling apart. The noise was deafening. Shocked and bruised, Tom realized that he was standing on the rocky outcrop where Etta had entered the caves. Now a new cave yawned where Tartok had smashed her way inside the mountain, but its mouth was steadily filling with falling rocks.

"This way!" Elenna grabbed Tom's arm.

But he pulled his arm from Elenna's grasp. "We have to go back," he said. "Tartok is still in there!"

Tom threw himself back toward the cave,

lifting his shield above his head for protection. Falling rocks bounced and shuddered against the sturdy wood. The rocks were already piled as high as Tom's shoulder, blocking Tartok's escape.

"It's impossible," Elenna shouted through the noise. "We have to leave, Tom! Etta has gone ahead. I promised we would follow —"

"No!" Tom yelled. "I won't leave Tartok. She helped me!"

He scrabbled at the rocks, throwing himself again and again at them. But it was a hopeless task. Tom could feel his courage failing.

He felt a hand on his shoulder. "I'm sorry, Tom," Elenna said. Silver stood at her side. "You're right. We have to save Tartok."

Storm whinnied and trotted over to nudge Tom on the shoulder. Stroking the stallion's neck, Tom stared at the blocked cave mouth.

"With all of us, we can do it," Tom said firmly.

Tom and Elenna threw themselves at the rocks.

They heaved and pulled, pushed and tugged. Silver nosed among the boulders, and Storm pounded at the rocks with his hooves. But nothing moved.

Help me, Aduro! Tom thought desperately. He had never needed the good wizard so much. But Aduro was in Malvel's grasp. He couldn't help them now.

Suddenly, there was a shimmer in the air behind Elenna. Tom stared, hardly daring to believe his eyes, as Aduro stepped onto the mountainside.

"There is no time for questions," Aduro said, holding up his hand. He looked gaunt, with dark circles beneath his eyes. Tom's heart ached for his friend.

"I have only a few moments before Malvel realizes I am missing," Aduro said. "You are doing well, Tom. Better than I could have hoped. Stay strong!"

The wizard raised his right hand and pointed at the rocks. He muttered some powerful magic words and there was a blast of white light. The rocks exploded. Storm whinnied in terror and Silver howled. Tom and Elenna fell to the ground and covered their eyes.

When they dared to open them, they saw that the rocks blocking the cave mouth had been blasted to powder. The entrance was open!

Tom whirled around to thank Aduro. To his horror, he saw the furious figure of Malvel grabbing the good wizard and dragging him away!

"You think you can defy me, Aduro?" Malvel roared. "I have been too patient with you. The pit of tar awaits!"

"No!" Tom shouted as Malvel's mocking laughter faded and Aduro vanished from sight. What had they done? Was this the end for their friend?

"Oh, Tom," Elenna choked. "Poor Aduro!"

They heard heavy footsteps. Tartok stepped out of the cave, blinking in the daylight. She was covered in dust, but otherwise looked as powerful as ever.

"Tartok!" Tom cried, overwhelmed with relief. "You're safe!"

The great Beast growled softly. She stretched out a massive white paw and laid it gently on Tom's head. Awestruck, Tom gazed into her fierce blue eyes.

The Beast threw out her chest and roared at the sky. Then she turned and walked away from Tom and his friends, climbing the mountainside with ease and grace — back to the snowy lands of the North.

Tom closed his eyes. Then he opened them again and stared at Elenna. She was smiling.

"Well done," she said. "You've conquered another Beast. Arachnid was truly evil."

Tom stroked his gleaming golden armor. Helmet, chain mail, breastplate, leg armor, and now the gauntlets. There was just one piece left — and one more Beast to fight. He had to stay strong. That glimpse of Malvel made Tom even more determined to rescue his friend before something awful could happen. With his friends, he would complete his Quest. And Malvel's power over Aduro would be broken.

Then came a familiar sound, which felt like a shard of ice in Tom's heart.

Malvel's laughter echoed around the broken mountainside. It bounced off the rocks and crevasses. Tom felt it wrap around him like Arachnid's web.

"So!" boomed the evil magician's voice. "You think you will defeat me? Your stupidity today nearly cost the life of one of Avantia's protectors. Is this Quest worth it?" His voice lowered to a whisper. *"Is it truly worth it?"*

Tom lifted his head. "While there's blood in my veins, I will defeat you, Malvel!" he shouted. He pulled his sword from its scabbard and pointed it to the sky. "We go to meet the final Beast!"